The sad c   her ani-
mals, he h

Changi   e autumn
leaves and   spring, in
the green

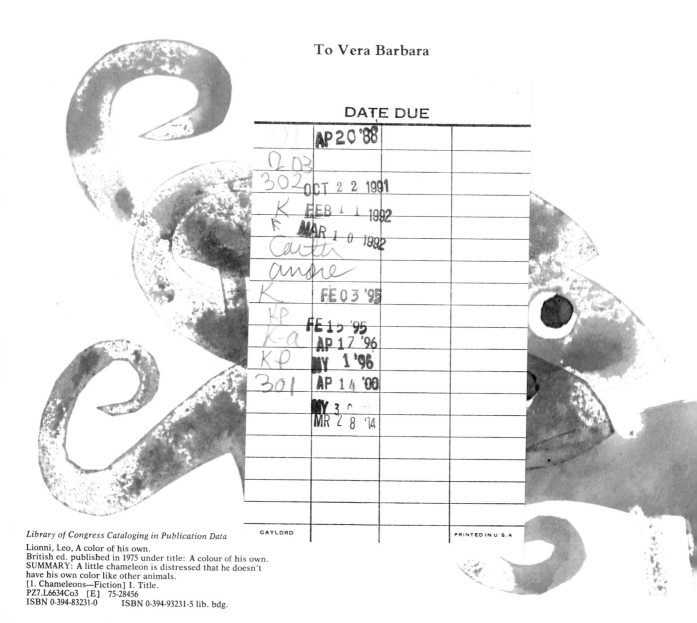

To Vera Barbara

DATE DUE

AP 20 '88		
OCT 2 2 1991		
FEB 1 1 1992		
MAR 1 0 1992		
FE 03 '95		
FE 15 '95		
AP 17 '96		
MY 1 '96		
AP 14 '00		
MY 3 ...		
MR 2 8 '14		

GAYLORD   PRINTED IN U.S.A.

Library of Congress Cataloging in Publication Data

Lionni, Leo, A color of his own.
British ed. published in 1975 under title: A colour of his own.
SUMMARY: A little chameleon is distressed that he doesn't
have his own color like other animals.
[1. Chameleons—Fiction] I. Title.
PZ7.L6634Co3 [E] 75-28456
ISBN 0-394-83231-0   ISBN 0-394-93231-5 lib. bdg.

A color of his own

Leo Lionni

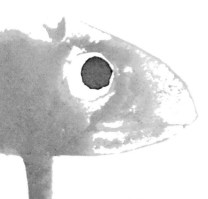

Pantheon Books

Parrots are green

goldfish are red

elephants are gray

pigs are pink.

All animals have a color of their own

except for chameleons.

They change color wherever they go.

On lemons they are yellow.

In the heather they are purple.

And on the tiger they are striped
like tigers.

One day a chameleon
who was sitting
on a tiger's tail
said to himself,

"If I remain on a leaf
I shall be green forever,
and so I too will have
a color of my own."

With this thought he cheerfully climbed
onto the greenest leaf.

But in autumn the leaf turned yellow
—and so did the chameleon.

Later the leaf turned red
and the chameleon too turned red.

And then
the winter winds
blew the leaf from
the branch
and with it
the chameleon

The chameleon was black in the long winter night.

But when spring came he walked out
into the green grass.
And there he met another chameleon.

He told his sad story.
"Won't we ever have a color
of our own?" he asked.

"I'm afraid not," said the other chameleon
who was older and wiser.
"But," he added,
"why don't we stay together?

We will still change color
wherever we go,
but you and I
will always be alike."

And so they remained side by side.

They were green together

and purple

and yellow

and red with white polka dots. And they lived happily

ever after.

Leo Lionni has created over a dozen animal fables, four of which—*Swimmy, Frederick, Alexander and the Wind-up Mouse,* and *Inch by Inch*—have been chosen as Caldecott Honor Books. His most recent books include *In The Rabbitgarden* and *Pezzettino,* the story of another small creature searching for his own special place in the world.

Born in Holland and educated in Italy, Mr. Lionni lived in this country for many years and now divides his time between New York and Italy. He is a former Art Director of *Fortune Magazine* and a past president of the American Institute of Graphic Arts, and was recently elected to the Art Directors Club Hall of Fame.